Thanksgiving Day at Our House

Thanksgiving Day at Our House

Thanksgiving Poems for the very young

Written by **Nancy White Carlstrom**

Illustrated by **R. W. Alley**

Aladdin Paperbacks
New York London Toronto Sydney Singapore

To the DeCoste family
Janet, Brad, Cara, Amy, and Lisa Renee
With love,
—N. W. C.

With thanks to those at our house,
Zoë, Cassandra, and Max
—R. W. A.

First Aladdin Paperbacks edition October 2002
Text copyright © 1999 by Nancy White Carlstrom
Illustrations copyright © 1999 by R. W. Alley

ALADDIN PAPERBACKS
An imprint of Simon & Schuster
Children's Publishing Division
1230 Avenue of the Americas
New York, NY 10020

Also available in a Simon & Schuster Books for Young Readers hardcover edition.
Designed by Anahid Hamparian
The text of this book was set in 17-point Green.
The illustrations were rendered in pen-and-ink and watercolor.
Printed in Hong Kong
2 4 6 8 10 9 7 5 3 1

The Library of Congress has cataloged the hardcover edition as follows:
Carlstrom, Nancy White
Thanksgiving Day at our house : Thanksgiving poems for the very young / written by Nancy White Carlstrom ; illustrated by R.W. Alley. –1st ed.
p. cm.
Summary: A collection of poems about one family's activities on Thanksgiving Day, including pondering the history behind the holiday, welcoming
visiting relatives, praying for others, enjoying the good food, and giving thanks at the end of the day.
ISBN 0-689-80360-5 (hc.)
1. Thanksgiving Day—Juvenile poetry. 2. Children's poetry, American. [1. Thanksgiving Day—Poetry. 2. American poetry.]
I. Alley, R. W. (Robert W.), ill. II. Title.
PS3553.A7355T47 1999
811'.54—dc21
98-49254
ISBN 0-689-85318-1 (Aladdin pbk.)

The Poems

The Day Before

All kinds of turkeys
   are strutting in the halls.
Finely feathered gobblers
   are squawking out their calls.

Pilgrim people rush around
   losing capes and hats.
Indians with their harvest feasts
   are dropping them on mats.

The day before Thanksgiving
   I really wouldn't miss.
We don't have any homework
   so let's give thanks for this!

K-1
Thanksgiving
Pageant

TODAY

The Mayflower

Over the water and over the waves
Sailing and sailing for many days

In a big, big ship
On a long, long trip

Were the people who came to America.

Onto the land and onto their knees
Thanks for bringing us over the seas

In a big, big ship
On a long, long trip

Said the people who came to America.

The First Thanksgiving

So many pumpkins
And so many beans.
More kinds of corn
Than we've ever seen—

In mush and in bread,
Roasted and dried;
Without Indian corn
We all would have died.

So thank you for corn
And thank you for friends.
On the earth and on others
We all must depend.

On Thanksgiving Day

This is the way the sky looks
    Gray gray gray
Will it rain, or will it snow
    On Thanksgiving Day?

This is the way the wind blows
    Leaves fly away
Winter whistles in the air
    On Thanksgiving Day.

    Is winter
        coming
            to dinner?

Rhyme Time Thanks

Thanks for

Roses
and noses and good smells

Stories to read
Stories to tell

Walking in the park
Night-light in the dark

Tying shoes at last
Running very fast

The moon and stars
Family close and family far

Brother
Mother

Sister
Whisper Love You

Father
Dad
Feeling glad

Grandma
Grandpa
Light and sound
When something lost is found
Like my pet bugs
Great big hugs
Chairs all sizes
Surprises

Knock Knock
Who can it be?
Open the door
It's our company!

More uncles
More aunts
and lots and lots of cousins.

The Way It Is at Our House

Do Uncle Ernie's socks match?
No! No! No!

Does Joey's little dog scratch?
So! So! So!

Does Granny Nan tell funny jokes?
Ho! Ho! Ho!

That's the way it is at our house
On Thanksgiving Day.

Does Auntie Kim wear ballet shoes?
Yes! Yes! Yes!

Does Grandpa's grace go on and on?
Bless! Bless! Bless!

And what do all the cousins do?
Mess! Mess! Mess!

That's the way it is at our house
On Thanksgiving Day.

Granny's Thanksgiving

Granny, tell us how it was when you were a girl.
Did you go over the river and through the woods?

I went down the river
On a big dogsled.
It was forty below
And our faces turned red.

Did you ever fall through?
Goodness no, child.
The ice was thick
But the ride was wild.

Slipping and sliding
All over the place—
The dogs thought it was
A Thanksgiving race.

By the end of our trip,
The pie was squashed.
The salad was frozen,
And the berries were tossed.

But what I remember
The most about
Was the heat of the stove
As we all thawed out.

Thanksgiving Parade

Boom baroom
Pum pum
Boom baroom
Tum tum

Beat the drum
Beat the drum
Make music in the Thanksgiving parade

Clickity click

Play the sticks

Ting-a-ling

Ping Ping

Tambourines shake
Shake shake shake
Make music in the Thanksgiving parade

Knock knock

The wooden blocks
Ring the bell
All is well

One two three four
March to the door
Make music in the Thanksgiving parade

Boom Knock
Ping
Shake

Make music in the Thanksgiving parade

Prayer for Others

God, help Grandma to get better
And my letter to get to her.

Help those without a home
To keep dry and warm.

Help those who are hungry
To have food that will fill them.

And help all lost dogs and children
To be found.

Thank You God for Bugs

Thank you God for
    marching ants
And bugs that dance
And roly-poly beetles
And all things small
That crawl.

Thanksgiving Charades

Sounds like wobble   gobble
Sounds like lurkey   turkey

Wobble gobble
Wobble gobble turkey

Sounds like wavy   gravy
Sounds like wash   squash
Sounds like bean please   green peas

Thick gravy
Wavy squash
Green peas
Please just one more.

Sounds like meat
Sounds like tomato
Sounds like eye

sweet
potato
pie

Sweet sweet sweet
Potato pie
My my my
It's time to eat!

Graces

Thanks for food that crunches
And grows in bunches
For food that mashes
And squishes and smashes

And tastes good going down.

The Quiet Moment

When the table is cleared
    and we've had enough,
All the cooks sit down,
    put their feet way up.
There's a short short time
    when it gets real still.
Of good food and good fun
    we have had our fill.

Listen then, you will hear
    plump babies on laps,
Snoring uncles, one aunt
    by the fire take naps.
Little dog curled up,
    big one stretched out,
Only whispers and sighs
    and not one shout.

It doesn't last long,
        but it plays a part.
It's good for the home.
It's good for the heart.

The quiet moment.

Thank-You Singing Game

Thank you for the sunshine
Thank you for the rain
Thank you for our family
Now let's play a game.

Around and around we go
Thanking as we sing
It's your turn to sing out thanks
Thanks for everything.

Babies
And how they grow
Cameras and photos
To help us remember
Other Thanksgivings
In other Novembers
Aunts and uncles
Cousins, friends
Work that starts
And work that ends
Food to eat
The sun for heat
Trees to climb
Special times
Like today
Laughter and play
Big things and little things
Anything and everything
We all together sing
Thank you.

Goodnight Prayer

Thank you, God, for everyone
Who made Thanksgiving Day so fun.

Thank you for our happy feast
For all things great and all things least.

Thank you for our life all year
For friends away and friends right here.

For family in all shapes and sizes
For what we know and for surprises.

Thanks for blankets
Lamps and toys
Thanks for Papa's singing noise.

Thanks for mama's kisses three
Thanks for you and thanks for me.